DESMOND BAGLEY

The Freedom
Trap

Fontana
An Imprint of HarperCollins*Publishers*

To Ron and Peggy Hulland

Fontana
An Imprint of HarperCollins*Publishers*
77–85 Fulham Palace Road,
Hammersmith, London W6 8JB

Published by Fontana 1971
30 29

First published in Great Britain by
Collins 1971

Copyright © Brockhurst Publications 1971

ISBN 0 00 615266 X

Set in Janson

Printed in Great Britain by
HarperCollinsManufacturing Glasgow

THE FREEDOM TRAP

Desmond Bagley was born in 1923 in Kendal, Westmorland, and brought up in Blackpool. He began his working life, aged 14, in the printing industry and then did a variety of jobs until going into an aircraft factory at the start of the Second World War.

When the war ended he decided to travel to southern Africa, going overland through Europe and the Sahara. He worked en route, reaching South Africa in 1951.

He became a freelance journalist in Johannesburg and wrote his first published novel, *The Golden Keel* in 1963. In 1964 he returned to England and lived in Totnes, Devon, for twelve years. He and his wife then moved to Guernsey in the Channel Islands. Here he found the ideal place for combining his writing with his other interests, which included computers, mathematics, military history, and entertaining friends from all over the world.

Desmond Bagley died in April 1983. *Juggernaut*, the second previously unpublished novel was published in June 1986: the first, *Night of Error*, was published in 1984 and was on the bestseller list for many weeks.

1

I

Mackintosh's office was, unexpectedly, in the City. I had difficulty in finding it because it was in that warren of streets between Holborn and Fleet Street which is a maze to one accustomed to the grid-iron pattern of Johannesburg. I found it at last in a dingy building; a well-worn brass plate announcing innocuously that this Dickensian structure held the registered office of Anglo-Scottish Holdings Ltd.

I smiled as I touched the polished plate, leaving a smudged fingerprint. It seemed that Mackintosh knew his business; this plate, apparently polished by generations of office boys, was a sign of careful planning that augured well for the future – the professional touch. I'm a professional and I don't like working with amateurs – they're unpredictable, careless and too dangerous for my taste. I had wondered about Mackintosh because England is the spiritual home of amateurism, but Mackintosh was a Scot and I suppose that makes a difference.

There was no lift, of course, so I trudged up four flights of stairs – poor lighting and marmalade-coloured walls badly in need of a repaint – and found the Anglo-Scottish office at the end of a dark corridor. It was all so normal that I wondered if I had the right address but I stepped forward to the desk and said, 'Rearden – to see Mr Mackintosh.'

The red-headed girl behind the desk favoured me with a warm smile and put down the tea-cup she was holding. 'He's expecting you,' she said. 'I'll see if he's free.' She went into the inner office, closing the door carefully behind her. She had good legs.

5

I looked at the scratched and battered filing cabinets and wondered what was in them and found I could not possibly guess. Perhaps they were stuffed full of Angles and Scots. There were two eighteenth-century prints on the wall – Windsor Castle and the Thames at Richmond. There was a Victorian steel engraving of Princes Street, Edinburgh. All very Anglic and Scottish. I admired Mackintosh more and more – this was going to be a good careful job; but I did wonder how he'd done it – did he call in an interior decorator or did he have a pal who was a set dresser in a film studio?

The girl came back. 'Mr Mackintosh will see you now – you can go right through.'

I liked her smile so I returned it and walked past her into Mackintosh's sanctum. He hadn't changed. I hadn't expected him to change – not in two months – but sometimes a man looks different on his home ground where he has a sense of security, a sense of knowing what's what. I was pleased Mackintosh hadn't changed in that way because it meant he would be sure of himself anywhere and at any time. I like people I can depend on.

He was a sand-coloured man with light gingery hair and invisible eyebrows and eyelashes which gave his face a naked look. If he didn't shave for a week probably no one would notice. He was slight in build and I wondered how he would use himself in a rough-house; flyweights usually invent nasty tricks to make up for lack of brawn. But then Mackintosh would never get into a brawl in the first place; there are all sorts of different ways of using your brains.

He put his hands flat on the desk. 'So you are,' he paused, holding his breath, and then spoke my name in a gasp, 'Rearden. And how was the flight, Mr Rearden?'

'Not bad.'

'That's fine. Sit down, Mr Rearden. Would you like some tea?' He smiled slightly. 'People who work in offices like this drink tea all the time.'

'All right,' I said, and sat down.

He went to the door. 'Could you rustle up another pot of tea, Mrs Smith?'

The door clicked gently as he closed it and I cocked my head in that direction. 'Does she know?'

'Of course,' he said calmly. 'I couldn't do without Mrs Smith. She's a very capable secretary, too.'

'Smith?' I asked ironically.

'Oh, it's her real name. Not too incredible – there are plenty of Smiths. She'll be joining us in a moment so I suggest we delay any serious discussion.' He peered at me. 'That's a rather lightweight suit for our English weather. You mustn't catch pneumonia.'

I grinned at him. 'Perhaps you'll recommend a tailor.'

'Indeed I will; you must go to my man. He's a bit expensive but I think we can manage that.' He opened a drawer and took out a fat bundle of currency. 'You'll need something for expenses.'

I watched unbelievingly as he began to count out the fivers. He parted with thirty of them, then paused. 'We'd better make it two hundred,' he decided, added another ten notes, then pushed the wad across to me. 'You don't mind cash, I trust? In my business cheques are rather looked down upon.'

I stuffed the money into my wallet before he changed his mind. 'Isn't this a little unusual? I didn't expect you to be so free and easy.'

'I daresay the expense account will stand it,' he said tolerantly. 'You are going to earn it, you know.' He offered a cigarette. 'And how was Johannesburg when you left?'

'Still the same in a changing sort of way,' I said. 'Since you were there they've built another hundred-and-sixty-foot office block in the city.'

'In two months? Not bad!'

'They put it up in twelve days,' I said drily.

'Go-ahead chaps, you South Africans. Ah, here's the tea.'

Mrs Smith put the tea tray on to the desk and drew up a chair. I looked at her with interest because anyone Mackintosh trusted was sure to be out of the ordinary. Not that she looked it, but perhaps that was because she was disguised as a secretary in a regulation twin-set – just another office girl with a nice smile. Yet in other circumstances I thought I could get on very well with Mrs Smith – in the absence of Mr Smith, of course.

Mackintosh waved his hand. 'Will you be Mother, Mrs Smith?' She busied herself with the cups, and Mackintosh said, 'There's no real need for further introductions, is there? You won't be around long enough for anything but the job, Rearden. I think we can get down to cases now.'

I winked at Mrs Smith. 'A pity.'

She looked at me unsmilingly. 'Sugar?' was all she asked.

He tented his fingers. 'Did you know that London is the world centre of the diamond business?'

'No, I didn't. I thought it was Amsterdam.'

'That's where the cutting is done. London is where diamonds are bought and sold in all stages of manufacture from uncut stones to finished pieces of jewellery.' He smiled. 'Last week I was in a place where packets of diamonds are sold like packets of butter in a grocer's shop.'

I accepted a cup of tea from Mrs Smith. 'I bet they have bags of security.'

'Indeed they have,' said Mackintosh. He held his arms wide like a fisherman describing the one that got away. 'The safe doors are that thick and the place is wired up with so many electronic gimmicks that if you blink an eyelash in the wrong place at the wrong time half the metropolitan police begin to move in.'

I sipped the tea, then put down the cup. 'I'm not a safe cracker,' I said. 'And I wouldn't know where to begin –

you need a peterman for that. Besides, it would have to be a team job.'

'Rest easy,' said Mackintosh. 'It was the South African angle that set me thinking about diamonds. Diamonds have all the virtues; they're relatively anonymous, portable and easily sold. Just the thing a South African would go for, don't you think? Do you know anything about the IDB racket?'

I shook my head. 'Not my line of country – so far.'

'It doesn't matter; perhaps it's for the better. You're a clever thief, Rearden; that's why you've stayed out of trouble. How many times have you been inside?'

I grinned at him. 'Once – for eighteen months. That was a long time ago.'

'Indeed it was. You change your methods and your aims, don't you? You don't leave any recurring statistics for a computer to sort out – no definite *modus operandi* to trip over. As I say – you're a clever thief. I think that what I have in mind will be just up your street. Mrs Smith thinks so, too.'

'Let's hear about it,' I said cautiously.

'The British GPO is a marvellous institution,' said Mackintosh inconsequentially. 'Some say ours is the best postal system in the world; some think otherwise if you judge by the readers' letters in the *Daily Telegraph*, but grousing is an Englishman's privilege. Insurance companies, however, regard the GPO very highly. Tell me, what is the most outstanding property of the diamond?'

'It sparkles.'

'An uncut diamond doesn't,' he pointed out. 'An uncut stone looks like a bit of sea-washed bottle glass. Think again.'

'It's hard,' I said. 'Just about the hardest thing there is.'

Mackintosh clicked his tongue in annoyance. 'He's not thinking, is he, Mrs Smith? Tell him.'

'The size – or the lack of it,' she said quietly.

Mackintosh pushed his hand under my nose and curled his fingers into a fist. 'You can hold a fortune in your hand and no one would know it was there. You could put diamonds worth a hundred thousand pounds into this matchbox – then what would you have?'

'You tell me.'

'You'd have a parcel, Rearden; a package. Something that can be wrapped up in brown paper with enough room to write an address and accept a postage stamp. Something that can be popped into a letter-box.'

I stared at him. 'They send diamonds through the *post*!'

'Why not? The postal system is highly efficient and very rarely is anything lost. Insurance companies are willing to bet large sums of money on the efficiency of the GPO and those boys know what they're doing. It's a matter of statistics, you know.'

He toyed with the matchbox. 'At one time there was a courier system and that had a lot of disadvantages. A courier would personally carry a parcel of diamonds and deliver it to its destination by hand. That fell through for a number of reasons; the couriers got to be known by the wide boys, which was very sad because a number of them were severely assaulted. Another thing was that human beings are but human, after all, and a courier could be corrupted. The supply of trustworthy men isn't bottomless and the whole courier system was not secure. Far from it.

'But consider the present system,' he said enthusiastically. 'Once a parcel is swallowed into the maw of the Post Office not even God can extract it until it reaches its destination. And why? Because nobody knows precisely where the hell it is. It's just one of millions of parcels circulating through the system and to find it would *not* be like finding a needle in a haystack – it would be like searching a haystack for a particular wisp of hay. Do you follow me?'

I nodded. 'It sounds logical.'

'Oh, it is,' said Mackintosh. 'Mrs Smith did all the necessary research. She's a very clever girl.' He flapped his hand languidly. 'Carry on, Mrs Smith.'

She said coolly, 'Once the insurance company actuaries analysed the GPO statistics regarding losses, they saw they were on to a good thing providing certain precautions were taken. To begin with, the stones are sent in all sizes and shapes of parcel from matchbox size to crates as big as a tea chest. The parcels are labelled in a multitude of different ways, very often with the trade label of a well-known firm – anything to confuse the issue, you see. The most important thing is the anonymity of the destination. There are a number of accommodation addresses having nothing to do with the diamond industry to which the stones are sent, and the same address is never used twice running.'

'Very interesting,' I said. 'Now how do we crack it?'

Mackintosh leaned back in his chair and put his fingertips together. 'Take a postman walking up a street – a familiar sight. He carries a hundred thousand pounds' worth of diamonds but – and this is the interesting point – he doesn't know it and neither does anyone else. Even the recipient who is eagerly awaiting the diamonds doesn't know when they'll arrive because the Post Office doesn't guarantee delivery at any specific time, regardless of what they say about first-class post in their specious advertising. The parcels are sent by ordinary post; no special delivery nonsense which would be too easy to crack open.'

I said slowly, 'It seems to me that you're painting yourself into a corner, but I suppose you have something up your sleeve. All right – I'll buy it.'

'Have you ever done any photography?'

I resisted the impulse to explode. This man had more ways of talking around a subject than anyone I had ever known. He had been the same in Johannesburg – never talking in a straight line for more than two minutes. 'I've clicked a shutter once or twice,' I said tightly.

'Black-and-white or colour?'

'Both.'

Mackintosh looked pleased. 'When you take colour photographs – transparencies – and send them away for processing, what do you get back?'

I looked appealingly at Mrs Smith and sighed. 'Small pieces of film with pictures on them.' I paused and added, 'They're framed in cardboard mounts.'

'What else do you get?'

'Nothing.'

He wagged his finger. 'Oh yes, you do. You get the distinctive yellow box the things are packed in. Yes, yellow – I suppose it could be described as Kodak yellow. If a man is carrying one of those boxes in his hand you can spot it across a street and you say to yourself, "That man is carrying a box of Kodachrome transparencies."'

I felt a thrill of tension. Mackintosh was coming to the meat of it. 'All right,' he said abruptly. 'I'll lay it out for you. I know when a parcel of diamonds is being sent. I know to where it is being sent – I have the accommodation address. Most important of all, I know the packaging and it's unmistakable. All you have to do is to wait near the address and the postman will come up to you with the damn thing in his hand. And that little yellow box will contain one hundred and twenty thousand quid in unset stones which you will take from him.'

'How did you find out all this?' I asked curiously.

'I didn't,' he said. 'Mrs Smith did. The whole thing is her idea. She came up with the concept and did all the research. Exactly *how* she did the research is no concern of yours.'

I looked at her with renewed interest and discovered that her eyes were green. There was a twinkle in them and her lips were curved in a humorous quirk which smoothed out as she said soberly, 'There must be as little violence as possible, Mr Rearden.'

'Yes,' agreed Mackintosh. 'As little violence as possible commensurate with making a getaway. I don't believe in violence; it's bad for business. You'd better bear that in mind.'

I said, 'The postman won't hand it to me. I'll have to take it by force.'

Mackintosh showed his teeth in a savage grin. 'So it will be robbery with violence if you get nabbed. Her Majesty's judges are hard about that kind of thing, especially considering the amount involved. You'll be lucky to get away with ten years.'

'Yes,' I said thoughtfully, and returned his grin with interest.

'Still, we won't make it too easy for the police. The drill is this; I'll be nearby and you'll keep on going. The stones will be out of the country within three hours of the snatch. Mrs Smith, will you attend to the matter of the bank?'

She opened a folder and produced a form which she pushed across the desk. 'Fill that in.'

It was a request to open an account at the *Züricher Ausführen Handelsbank*. Mrs Smith said, 'British politicians may not like the gnomes of Zürich but they come in handy when needed. Your number is very complicated – write it out fully in words in this box.'

Her finger rested on the form so I scribbled the number in the place she indicated. She said, 'That number written on the right cheque form in place of a signature will release to you any amount of money up to forty thousand pounds sterling, or its equivalent in any currency you wish.'

Mackintosh sniggered. 'Of course, you'll have to get the diamonds first.'

I stared at them. 'You're taking two-thirds.'

'I did plan it,' Mrs Smith said coolly.

Mackintosh grinned like a hungry shark. 'She has expensive tastes.'

'Of that I have no doubt,' I said. 'Would your tastes run

to a good lunch? You'll have to suggest a restaurant, though; I'm a new boy in London.'

She was about to answer when Mackintosh said sharply, 'You're not here to play footsie with my staff, Rearden. It wouldn't be wise for you to be seen with either of us. Perhaps when it's all over we can have dinner together – the three of us.'

'Thanks,' I said bleakly.

He scribbled on a piece of paper. 'I suggest that after lunch you . . . er . . . "case the joint" – I believe that is the correct expression. Here is the address of the drop.' He pushed the paper across the desk, and scribbled again. 'And this is the address of my tailor. Don't get them mixed up, there's a good chap. That would be disastrous.'

II

I lunched at the Cock in Fleet Street and then set out to look up the address Mackintosh had given me. Of course I walked in the wrong direction – London is the devil of a place to get around in if you don't know it. I didn't want to take a taxi because I always play things very cautiously, perhaps even too cautiously. But that's why I'm a success.

Anyway, I found myself walking up a street called Ludgate Hill before I found I'd gone wrong and, in making my way into Holborn, I passed the Central Criminal Court. I knew it was the Central Criminal Court, because it says so and that surprised me because I always thought it was called the Old Bailey. I recognized it because of the golden figure of Justice on the roof. Even a South African would recognize that – we see Edgar Lustgarten movies, too.

It was all very interesting but I wasn't there as a tourist so I passed up the opportunity of going inside to see if there was a case going on. Instead I pressed on to Leather Lane

14

behind Gamage's and found a street market with people selling all kinds of junk from barrows. I didn't much like the look of that – it's difficult to get away fast in a thick crowd. I'd have to make damned sure there was no hue and cry, which meant slugging the postman pretty hard. I began to feel sorry for him.

Before checking on the address I cruised around the vicinity, identifying all the possible exits from the area. To my surprise I found that Hatton Garden runs parallel with Leather Lane and I knew that the diamond merchants hung out there. On second thoughts it wasn't too surprising; the diamond boys wouldn't want their accommodation address to be too far from the ultimate destination. I looked at the stolid, blank buildings and wondered in which of them were the strongrooms Mackintosh had described.

I spent half an hour pacing out those streets and noting the various types of shop. Shops are very useful to duck into when you want to get off the streets quickly. I decided that Gamage's might be a good place to get lost in and spent another quarter-hour familiarizing myself with the place. That wouldn't be enough but at this stage it wasn't a good thing to decide definitely on firm plans. That's the trouble with a lot of people who slip up on jobs like this; they make detailed plans too early in the game, imagining they're Master Minds, and the whole operation gets hardening of the arteries and becomes stiff and inflexible.

I went back to Leather Lane and found the address Mackintosh had given me. It was on the second floor, so I went up to the third in the creaking lift and walked down one flight of stairs. The Betsy-Lou Dress Manufacturing Co. Ltd was open for business but I didn't trouble to introduce myself. Instead I checked the approaches and found them reasonably good, although I would have to observe the postman in action before I could make up my mind about the best way of doing the job.

I didn't hang about too long, just enough to take rough

bearings, and within ten minutes I was back in Gamage's and in a telephone booth. Mrs Smith must have been literally hanging on to the telephone awaiting my call because the bell rang only once before she answered, 'Anglo-Scottish Holdings.'

'Rearden,' I said.

'I'll put you through to Mr Mackintosh.'

'Wait a minute,' I said. 'What kind of a Smith are you?'

'What do you mean?'

'Don't you have a first name?'

There was a pause before she said, 'Perhaps you'd better call me Lucy.'

'Ouch! I don't believe it.'

'You'd better believe it.'

'Is there a Mr Smith?'

Frost formed on the earpiece of my telephone as she said icily, 'That's no business of yours. I'll put you through to Mr Mackintosh.'

There was a click and the line went dead temporarily and I thought I wasn't much of a success as a great lover. It wasn't surprising really; I couldn't see Lucy Smith – if that was her name – wanting to enter into any kind of close relationship with me until the job was over. I felt depressed.

Mackintosh's voice crackled in my ear. 'Hello, dear boy.'

'I'm ready to talk about it some more.'

'Are you? Well, come and see me tomorrow at the same time.'

'All right,' I said.

'Oh, by the way, have you been to the tailor yet?'

'No.'

'You'd better hurry,' he said. 'There'll be the measurements and at least three fittings. You'll just about have time to get it all in before you get slapped in the nick.'

'Very funny,' I said, and slammed down the phone. It was all right for Mackintosh to make snide comments; he wasn't going to do the hard work. I wondered what else he did in that shabby office apart from arranging diamond robberies.

I took a taxi into the West End and found Austin Reed's, where I bought a very nice reversible weather coat and one of those caps as worn by the English country gent, the kind in which the cloth crown is sewn on to the peak. They wanted to wrap the cap but I rolled it up and put it into the pocket of the coat which I carried out over my arm.

I didn't go near Mackintosh's tailor.

III

'So you think it's practicable,' said Mackintosh.

I nodded. 'I'll want to know a bit more, but it looks all right so far.'

'What do you want to know?'

'Number one – when is the job to be?'

Mackintosh grinned. 'The day after tomorrow,' he said airily.

'Christ!' I said. 'That's not allowing much time.'

He chuckled. 'It'll be all over in less than a week after you've set foot in England.' He winked at Mrs Smith. 'It's not everyone who can make forty thousand quid for a week's not very hard work.'

'I can see at least one other from here,' I said sarcastically. 'I don't see that you're working your fingers to the bone.'

He was undisturbed. 'Organization – that's my forte.'

'It means I've got to spend the rest of today and all tomorrow studying the habits of the British postman,' I said. 'How many deliveries a day?'

Mackintosh cocked his eye at Mrs Smith, who said, 'Two.'

'Have you any snoopers you can recruit? I don't want to spend too much time around Leather Lane myself. I might

17

get picked up for loitering and that would certainly queer the pitch.'

'It's all been done,' said Mrs Smith. 'I have the timetable here.'

While I was studying it, she unrolled a plan on to the desk. 'This is a plan of the entire second floor. We're lucky on this one. In some buildings there's a row of letter-boxes in the entrance hall, but not here. The postman delivers to every office.'

Mackintosh put down his finger with a stabbing motion. 'You'll tackle the postman just about here. He'll have the letters for that damnably named clothing company in his hand ready for delivery and you ought to see whether he's carrying the package or not. If he isn't you pass it up and wait for the next delivery.'

'That's what's worrying me,' I said. 'The waiting bit. If I'm not careful I'll stick out like a sore thumb.'

'Oh, didn't I tell you – I've rented an office on the same floor,' said Mackintosh blandly. 'Mrs Smith went shopping and all home comforts are installed; an electric kettle, tea, coffee, sugar and milk, and a basket of goodies from Fortnum's. You'll live like a king. I hope you like caviare.'

I blew out my breath sharply. 'Don't bother to consult me about anything,' I said sarcastically, but Mackintosh merely smiled and tossed a key-ring on the desk. I picked it up. 'What name am I trading under?'

'Kiddykar Toys Limited,' said Mrs Smith. 'It's a genuine company.'

Mackintosh laughed. 'I set it up myself – cost all of twenty-five quid.'

We spent the rest of the morning scheming and I didn't find any snags worth losing any sleep over. I found myself liking Lucy Smith more and more; she had a brain as sharp as a razor and nothing escaped her attention, and yet she contrived to retain her femininity and avoid bossiness, something that seems difficult for brainy women. When we

18

had just about got everything wrapped up, I said, 'Come now; Lucy isn't your real name. What is?'

She looked at me with clear eyes. 'I don't think it really matters,' she said evenly.

I sighed. 'No,' I admitted. 'Perhaps not.'

Mackintosh regarded us with interest, then said abruptly, 'I said there was to be no lally-gagging around with the staff, Rearden; you just stick to doing your job.' He looked at his watch. 'You'd better leave now.'

So I left the gloom of his nineteenth-century office and lunched again at the Cock, and the afternoon was spent in the registered office of Kiddykar Toys Ltd, two doors away from the Betsy-Lou Dress Manufacturing Co. Ltd. Everything was there that Mackintosh had promised, so I made myself a pot of coffee and was pleased to see that Mrs Smith had supplied the real stuff and not the instant powdered muck.

There was a good view of the street and, when I checked on the timetable of the postman, I was able to identify his route. Even without the telephone call Mackintosh was to make I ought to get at least fifteen minutes' notice of his arrival. That point settled, I made a couple of expeditions from the office, pacing the corridor and timing myself. There really was no point in doing it without knowledge of the postman's speed but it was good practice. I timed myself from the office to Gamage's, walking at a fair clip but not so fast as to attract attention. An hour in Gamage's was enough to work out a good confusing route and then work was over for the day and I went back to my hotel.

The next day was pretty much the same except I had the postman to practise on. The first delivery I watched from the office with the door opened a crack and a stopwatch in my hand. That might seem a bit silly; after all, all I had to do was to cosh a man. But there was a hell of a lot at stake so I went through the whole routine.

On the second delivery of the day I did a dummy run on

the postman. Sure enough, it was as Mackintosh had predicted; as he approached Betsy-Lou's door the letters for delivery were firmly clutched in hand and any box of Kodachromes should be clearly visible. I hoped Mackintosh was right about the diamonds; we'd look mighty foolish if we ended up with a photographic record of Betsy-Lou's weekend in Brighton.

Before I left I telephoned Mackintosh and he answered the telephone himself. I said, 'I'm as ready as I'll ever be.'

'Good!' He paused. 'You won't see me again – apart from the hand-over of the merchandise tomorrow. Make a neat job of that, for God's sake!'

'What's the matter?' I asked. 'Got the wind up?'

He didn't answer that one. Instead, he said, 'You'll find a present awaiting you at your hotel. Handle with care.' Another pause. 'Good luck.'

I said, 'Give my sincere regards to Mrs Smith.'

He coughed. 'It wouldn't do, you know.'

'Perhaps not; but I like to make my own decisions.'

'Maybe so – but she'll be in Switzerland tomorrow. I'll pass on your message when I next see her.' He rang off.

I went back to the hotel, picked up a small package at the desk, and unwrapped it in my room. Nestling in a small box was a cosh, lead-centered and rubber-padded with a non-skid grip and a neat strap to go round the wrist. A very effective anaesthetic instrument, if a bit more dangerous than most. Also in the box was a scrap of paper with a single line of typescript: HARD ENOUGH AND NO HARDER.

I went to bed early that night. There was work to do next day.

IV

Next morning I went into the City like any other business gent, although I didn't go so far as to wear a bowler and carry the staff of office – the rolled umbrella. I was earlier than most because the first postal delivery of the day was before office hours. I arrived at Kiddykar Toys with half an hour in hand and immediately put on the kettle for coffee before inspecting the view from the window. The stallholders of Leather Lane were getting ready for the day's sales and there was no sign of Mackintosh. I wasn't worried; he'd be around somewhere in the neighbourhood keeping an eye open for the postman.

I had just finished the first cup of coffee when the phone rang. Mackintosh said briefly, 'He's coming.' There was a click as he hung up.

In the interests of his leg muscles the postman had put in a bit of time and motion study on this building. It was his habit to take the lift to the top floor and deliver the letters from the top down on the theory that walking downstairs is easier than climbing them. I put on my coat and hat and opened the door a couple of inches, listening for the whine of the lift. It was ten minutes before I heard it go up, and then I stepped out into the corridor, carefully drawing the office door closed but not quite shut so that the least push would swing it open.

It was very quiet in the building at that hour and, as I heard the postman clattering down the stairs to the second floor, I retreated down the flight of stairs to the first floor. He hit the second floor and turned away from Betsy-Lou's door to deliver the post to other offices. That was his usual routine and so I wasn't worried.

Then I heard him coming back a few steps at a time, the

intervals punctuated by the metallic bangs of swinging letterbox flaps. Just at the right time I came up the stairs and headed for the Kiddykar office which brought me facing him. I stared at his hands but there was no little yellow box to be seen.

'Morning,' he said. 'Lovely day, isn't it?' He went past at a quick pace and I fumbled my way into the office, faking the opening of the door with a key. As I closed it behind me I found that I was sweating slightly; not much but enough to show that I was under tension. It was ridiculous, I suppose – I had only to take a little box away from an unsuspecting man, which should have been the easiest thing in the world and no occasion for nerves.

It was the contents of that box which set up the tension. A hundred and twenty thousand quid is a hell of a lot of money to be at stake. It's rather like the man who can walk along a kerbstone unconcernedly and never put a foot wrong, yet let him try the same thing with a two-hundred-foot drop on one side and he'll break into a muck sweat.

I walked over to the window and opened the casement, not so much to get fresh air as to signal to Mackintosh that the first delivery was a bust. I looked down into Leather Lane and saw him in his appointed place. He was standing before a fruit and vegetable stall prodding tomatoes with a nervous forefinger. He flicked his eyes up at the window then swung around and walked away.

I lit a cigarette and settled down with the morning papers. There was quite a while to wait before the second post.

Two hours later the telephone rang again. 'Better luck this time,' said Mackintosh, and hung up.

I went through the same routine as before – there was no harm in it as this would be a different postman. I waited on the landing just below the second floor and listened intently. It would be more difficult now that the building was inhabited and a lot depended on whether I could catch the postman alone in the corridor. If I could then it was easy, but if there was anyone else present I would have to grab the box and run for it.

Steady footsteps warned me that he was coming and I trotted up the stairs at the critical moment. I swung my head back and forwards like someone about to cross a street, and found that all was clear – no one in the corridor except for me and the postman. Then I looked at his hands.

He was carrying a bundle of letters and right on top of the bundle was a little yellow box.

I stepped right in front of him as he drew abreast of the Kiddykar office. 'Have you anything for me?' I asked. 'I'm in there.' I pointed to the door behind him.

He turned his head to look at the name on the door and I hit him behind the ear with the cosh, hoping to God he hadn't an unusually thin skull. He grunted and his knees buckled. I caught him before he fell and pushed him at the door of the office which swung open under his weight, and he fell over the threshold spilling letters before him. The Kodachrome box fell to the floor with a little thump.

I stepped over him and hauled him inside, pushing the door closed with my foot. Then I grabbed the yellow box and dropped it into the innocuous brown box that Mackintosh had had specially tailored to fit it. I had to pass it on to him in the street and we wanted no flash of that conspicuous yellow to be seen.

In less than sixty seconds from the time I greeted the postman I was outside the office and locking the door on him. As I did so someone passed behind me in the corridor and opened the door of the Betsy-Lou office. I turned and went downstairs, not moving too fast but not dawdling. I reckoned the postman wouldn't come round for two or three minutes, and then he still had to get out of the office.

I came out on to the street and saw Mackintosh staring at me. He averted his eyes and half-turned away and I strode across the street among the stalls in his direction. It was easy enough, in the throng, to bump him with my shoulder, and with a muffled 'Sorry!' I passed the packet to him and continued in the direction of Holborn.

I hadn't gone far when I heard the smash of glass behind me and a confused shouting. That postman had been smart; he had wasted no time on the door but had broken the window as a means of drawing attention to himself. Also he hadn't been unconscious for as long as I had hoped – I hadn't hit him nearly hard enough.

But I was safe – far enough away not to be spotted by him and moving farther all the time. It would take at least five minutes to sort out the confusion and by that time I intended to get thoroughly lost – and I hoped Mackintosh was doing the same. He was the hot one now – he had the diamonds.

I ducked into the rear entrance of Gamage's and made my way through the store at an easier pace, looking, I hoped, like a man who knows where he's going. I found the men's room and locked myself into a cubicle. My coat came off and was reversed – that so carefully chosen coat with the nicely contrasting colours. The natty cap came from my pocket and the hat I was wearing was regretfully screwed into a shapeless bundle. It wouldn't do it much good to be jammed into my pocket but I didn't want to leave it lying around.

Clothes make the man and a new man left that men's room. I wandered casually about the store, drifting towards the front entrance, and on the way I bought myself a new tie just to have a legitimate reason for being in Gamage's, but that precaution was unnecessary. I emerged on to the pavement of Holborn and set off to walk west. No taxis for me because taxi-drivers would be questioned about pick-ups in the area at that time.

Half an hour later I was in a pub just off Oxford Street near the Marble Arch and sinking a thankful pint of beer.

It had been a good smooth job but it wasn't over yet, not by a hell of a long way. I wondered if I could trust Mackintosh to do his half of the job properly.

V

That evening, as I was preparing to go out on the town, there came a firm knock at the door of my room. I opened it and was confronted by two very large men dressed very conservatively and in the best of taste. The one on the right said, 'Are you Joseph Aloysius Rearden?'

I didn't have to bend my brain too far to realize that these two were coppers. I gave a twisted grin. 'I'd rather forget the Aloysius.'

'We are police officers.' He flipped a wallet in front of me negligently. 'We hope you can assist us in our enquiries.'

'Hey!' I said. 'Is that a warrant card? I've never seen one of those before.'

Reluctantly he flipped open the wallet again and let me read the card. He was Detective-Inspector John M. Brunskill and indubitably the genuine article. I babbled a bit. 'You see these things happening at the bioscope; I never thought it would happen to me.'

'Bioscope?' he said dubiously.

'The films – we call a cinema a bioscope in South Africa. That's where I'm from, you know. I don't know how I can help you in any enquiries, Inspector. I'm a stranger to London – in fact, I'm a stranger to England. I've been here only a week – less than that, really.'

'We know all that, Mr Rearden,' said Brunskill gently.

So they'd checked on me already. These boys moved fast – the British police are wonderful.

'May we come in, Mr Rearden? I think you *will* be able to help us.'

I stood on one side and waved them into the room.

'Come in and take a seat. There's only one chair so one of you will have to sit on the bed. And take your coats off.'

'That won't be necessary,' said Brunskill. 'We won't be staying long. This is Detective-Sergeant Jervis.'

Jervis looked an even harder nut than Brunskill. Brunskill was polished and had the suavity that maturity brings, while Jervis still had his sharp corners and was all young, rock-hard cop. But Brunskill would be the more dangerous – he'd be tricky.

I said, 'Well, what can I do for you?'

'We are making enquiries about the theft of a package from a postman in Leather Lane this morning,' said Brunskill. 'What can you tell us about it, Mr Rearden?'

'Where's Leather Lane?' I asked. 'I'm a stranger here.'

Brunskill looked at Jervis and Jervis looked at Brunskill and then they both looked at me. 'Come, Mr Rearden,' said Brunskill. 'You can do better than that.'

'You've got a record,' said Jervis suddenly.

This was the shot across the bows. I said bitterly, 'And you johns will never let me forget it. Yes, I've got a record; I did eighteen months in Pretoria Central – eighteen months of stone cold jug – and that was a long time ago. I've been straight ever since.'

'Until perhaps this morning,' suggested Brunskill.

I looked him straight in the eye. 'Don't pull the old flannel on me. You tell me what I'm supposed to have done, and I'll tell you if I did it – straight out.'

'Very good of you,' murmured Brunskill. 'Don't you think so, Sergeant?'

Jervis made a nasty noise at the back of his throat. Then he said, 'Mind if we search your room, Rearden?'

'It's Mr Rearden to sergeants,' I said. 'Your boss has better manners than you. And I most certainly do object to you searching my room – unless you have a warrant.'

'Oh, we have that,' said Brunskill calmly. 'Go ahead, Sergeant.' He took a document from his pocket and slapped

26

it into my hand. 'I think you'll find that in order, Mr Rearden.'

I didn't even bother to look at it, but just tossed it on to the dressing-table and watched Jervis do an efficient overhaul of the room. He found nothing – there wasn't anything for him to find. At last he gave up, looked at Brunskill and shook his head.

Brunskill turned to me. 'I must ask you to come to the police station with me.'

I was silent and let the pause lengthen for a long time before I said, 'Well, go ahead and ask.'

'We've got ourselves a joker here, sir,' said Jervis. He looked at me with dislike.

'If you do ask I won't come,' I said. 'You'll have to arrest me to get me anywhere near the nick.'

Brunskill sighed. 'Very well, Mr Rearden; I arrest you on suspicion of being involved in an assault on a postman on premises in Leather Lane at about nine-thirty this morning. Does that satisfy you?'

'It'll do to be going on with,' I said. 'Let's go.'

'Oh, I almost forgot,' he said. 'Anything you say will be noted and may be used in evidence.'

'I know the form,' I said. 'I know it only too well.'

'I'm sure you do,' he said softly.

I expected them to take me to Scotland Yard but I found myself in quite a small police station. Where it was I don't know – I don't know London at all well. They put me into a small room unfurnished except for a deal table and two bentwood chairs. It had the same institutional smell of all police stations anywhere in the world. I sat in a chair and smoked one cigarette after another, watched by a uniformed copper who stood with his back to the door, looking undressed without his helmet.

It was nearly an hour and a half before they got around to doing anything and it was tough boy Jervis who started the attack. He came into the room and waved abruptly at the uniformed john who did a disappearing act, then he sat down at the other side of the table and looked at me for a long time without speaking. I ignored him – I didn't even look at him and it was he who broke first. 'You've been here before, haven't you, Rearden?'

'I've never been here before in my life.'

'You know what I mean. You've sat on hard wooden chairs with a policeman the other side of the table many, many times. You know the drill too well – you're a professional. With another man I might pussyfoot around – use a bit of psychology, maybe – but that wouldn't work with you, would it? So I'm not going to do it. There'll be no tact, no psychology with you. I'm going to crack you like a nut, Rearden.'

'You'd better remember Judges' Rules.'

He gave a sharp bark of laughter. 'See what I mean? An honest man wouldn't know Judges' Rules from Parkinson's Law. But you know, don't you? You're a wrong 'un; you're bent.'

'When you're finished with the insults I'll go,' I said.

'You'll go when I say you can,' he said sharply.

I grinned at him. 'You'd better check with Brunskill first, sonny.'

'Where are the diamonds?'

'What diamonds?'

'That postman is in a bad way. You hit him a bit too hard, Rearden. The chances are he'll cash in his chips – and where will that put you?' He leaned forward. 'You'll be inside for so long that you'll trip over your beard.'

I must say he was trying hard but he was a bad liar. No dying postman could have busted that window in the Kiddykar office. I just looked him in the eye and kept my mouth shut.

'If those diamonds aren't found it'll go hard for you,' said

Jervis. 'Maybe if the diamonds turn up the judge will be a bit easier on you.'

'What diamonds?' I asked.

And so it went on for a good half-hour until he got tired and went away and the uniformed man came back and took up his old stance in front of the door. I turned and looked at him. 'Don't you get corns? Isn't this job bad for your feet?' He looked at me with a bland face and expressionless eyes and said exactly nothing.

Presently a bigger gun was brought to bear. Brunskill came in carrying a thick folder bulging with papers which he put on the table. 'I'm sorry to have kept you waiting, Mr Rearden,' he said.

'I wouldn't like to bet on it,' I said.

He gave me a pitying, though understanding, smile. 'We all have our jobs to do, and some are nastier than others. You mustn't blame me for doing mine.' He opened the folder. 'You have quite a record, Mr Rearden. Interpol have a fat dossier on you.'

'I've been convicted once,' I said. 'Anything else is not official and you can't use it. What anyone might have to say about me isn't proof of a damned thing.' I grinned and, pointing at the folder, quoted: '"What the policeman said isn't evidence."'

'Just so,' said Brunskill. 'But it's interesting all the same.' He mused over the papers for a long time, then said, without looking up, 'Why are you flying to Switzerland tomorrow?'

'I'm a tourist,' I said. 'I've never been there before.'

'It's your first time in England, too, isn't it?'

'You know it is. Look here, I want an attorney.'

He looked up. 'I would suggest a solicitor. Have you anyone in mind?'

From my wallet I took the scrap of paper with the telephone number on it which Mackintosh had given me with this eventuality in mind. 'That'll find him,' I said.

Brunskill's eyebrows lifted when he read it. 'I know this number very well – he's just the man to tackle your type of case. For a man who's been in England less than a week you know your way around the fringes.' He put the paper on one side. 'I'll let him know you're here.'

My throat was dry from smoking too many cigarettes. 'Another thing,' I said. 'I could do with a cup of tea.'

'I'm afraid we can't run to tea,' said Brunskill regretfully. 'Would a glass of water be all right?'

'It'll do.'

He went to the door, gave instructions, and then came back. 'You people seem to think that we spend all our time in police stations drinking tea – running a continuous cafeteria for old lags. I can't think where you get it from unless it's from television.'

'Not me,' I said. 'We have no TV in South Africa.'

'Indeed!' said Brunskill. 'How curious. Now, about those diamonds. I think that . . .'

'What diamonds?' I broke in.

And so it went on. He shook me more than Jervis because he was trickier. He wasn't stupid enough to lie about something I knew to be true, as Jervis had done, and was better at the wearing down process, being as persistent as a buzzing fly. The water came – a carafe and a tumbler. I filled the tumbler and drank thirstily, then refilled it and drank again. Brunskill watched me and said at last, 'Had enough?'

I nodded, so he reached out and took the tumbler delicately in his fingertips and carried it out. When he came back he looked at me sorrowfully. 'I didn't think you'd fall for that chestnut. You know we can't fingerprint you until you're booked. Why did you let us have them?'

'I was tired,' I said.

'Too bad,' he said sympathetically. 'Now, to get back to those diamonds . . .'

* * *

Presently Jervis came into the room and beckoned to Brunskill and they stood by the door and talked in low voices. Brunskill turned around. 'Now, look here, Rearden; we've nailed you. We have enough evidence now to send you up for ten years. If you help us to get back those stones it might help you when the judge sentences you.'

'What diamonds?' I asked tiredly.

His mouth shut with a snap. 'All right,' he said curtly. 'Come this way.'

I followed, the meat in a sandwich between Brunskill and Jervis. They escorted me to a large room occupied by a dozen men lined along one wall. Jervis said, 'No need to explain what this is, Rearden; but I will because the law says I must. It's a line-up – an identification parade. There are three people coming in to see you. You can insert yourself anywhere in that line, and you can change your position in the intervals if you like. Got it?'

I nodded and walked over to the wall, putting myself third in line. There was a pause in the action and then the first witness came in – a little old lady, someone's darling mother. She went along the line and then came straight back to me and pointed at my chest. 'That's the one.' I'd never seen her before.

They took her out, but I didn't bother to change position. There wasn't any point, really; they had me nailed just as Brunskill had. The next one was a young man of about eighteen. He didn't have to go all the way along the line. He stopped in front of me. 'That's 'im,' he said. ' 'E did it.'

The third witness didn't have any trouble either. He took one look at me and yelled, 'This is the boyo. I hope you get life, mate.' He went away rubbing his head. It was the postman – not nearly as dead as Jervis would have me believe.

Then it was over and Jervis and Brunskill took me back. I said to Jervis, 'You'd make a good miracle-worker; you brought that postman back to life pretty smartly.'

He gave me a sharpish look and a slow smile spread over his face. 'And how did you know that was the postman?'

I shrugged. My goose was cooked whichever way I looked at it. I said to Brunskill, 'Who is the bastard of a nark that shopped me?'

His face closed up. 'Let's call it "information received", Rearden. You'll be charged tomorrow morning and you'll go before a magistrate immediately. I'll see that your solicitor is in attendance.'

'Thanks,' I said. 'What's his name?'

'By God!' he said. 'But you're a cool one. Your solicitor is a Mr Maskell.'

'Thanks again,' I said.

Brunskill whistled up a station sergeant who put me in a cell for the night. I had a bite to eat and then stretched out and went to sleep almost immediately.

It had been a tiring day.

2

I

Maskell was a short, stout man with shrewd brown eyes and an immense air of dignity. He was introduced to me just before the charge was laid and did not seem at all perturbed at the prospect of acting for a criminal. The law is a strange profession in which ordinary morality goes by the board; a well liked and generally respected barrister will fight like a tiger for his client, who may well be a murderer or a rapist, and will receive well-merited congratulations on an acquittal. Then he will go home and write a letter to the editor of *The Times* fulminating about the rise in crime. A schizophrenic profession.

I said as much to Maskell once when I knew him better. He said gently, 'Mr Rearden, to me you are neither guilty nor innocent – the people who decide that are the twelve men in the box. I am here to find out the facts in a case and to present them to a barrister who will conduct the argument – and I do it for money.'

We were in court at the time and he waved his hand largely. 'Who says crime doesn't pay?' he asked cynically. 'Taking all in all, from the court ushers to his Lordship up there, there are at least fifty people directly involved in this case, and they're all making a living out of it. Some, such as myself and his Lordship, make a better living than others. We do very well out of people like you, Mr Rearden.'

But at this time I didn't know Maskell at all. It was a hurried introduction, and he said hastily, 'We will talk in more detail later. First we must find what this is all about.'

So I was taken and charged. I won't go into all the legal

language but what it all boiled down to was robbery with violence – an assault on the person of John Edward Harte, an employee of the GPO, and the theft of diamonds, the property of Lewis and van Veldenkamp Ltd, valued at £173,000.

I nearly burst out laughing at that. It had been a bigger haul than Mackintosh had expected, unless Mr Lewis and Meneer van Veldenkamp were trying to sting their insurance company. But I kept a straight face and when it was over I turned to Maskell and asked, 'What now?'

'I'll see you in the Magistrates' Court in about an hour. That will be a mere formality.' He rubbed his chin. 'There's a lot of money involved here. Have the police recovered the diamonds?'

'You'd better ask them. I know nothing about any diamonds.'

'Indeed! I must tell you that if the diamonds are still – shall we say *at large*? – then it will be very difficult for me to get you out on bail. But I will try.'

The proceedings in the Magistrates' Court were brief, lasting for about three minutes. They would have been even briefer but Brunskill got on his hind legs and argued against the granting of bail. 'The diamonds have not yet been recovered, your Honour, and if the prisoner is released on bail I fear they never will be. Further, if the prisoner had not been apprehended last night he would have been in Switzerland this morning.'

The magistrate flapped his hand. 'You think the prisoner will jump bail?'

'I do,' said Brunskill firmly. 'And there is one thing more, the prisoner is in the dock on a charge of violence and he has a police record in which violence figures largely. I fear the intimidation of witnesses.'

He nearly overreached himself. 'You think he will leave the country *and* intimidate witnesses?' asked the magistrate with polite incredulity. 'I doubt if his violent arm would reach so far. However, on the balance of evidence and especially in respect of the missing property I am inclined to agree with you. Bail is denied.'

Brunskill sat down and Maskell shrugged and stuffed some papers back into his briefcase. And so I was remanded for trial at the Central Criminal Court. I was going to see the inside of the Old Bailey, after all.

Maskell had a few words with me before I was taken away. 'Now I can find out the strength of the police case against you. I'll have a word with the prosecution and then you and I can sit down together and discuss this whole thing. If you want anything ask that I be informed, but I shall probably see you tomorrow, anyway.'

A prisoner on remand is theoretically an innocent man. Practically, he is regarded neutrally as neither guilty nor innocent. The food was good, the bed soft and there were no irksome restrictions – except one. I couldn't get out of the nick. Still, you can't have everything.

Maskell came to see me the following afternoon and we sat in one of the interviewing rooms. He regarded me thoughtfully, then said, 'The case against you is very strong, Mr Rearden; very strong, indeed. Unless you can prove conclusively and without equivocation that you could not have committed this crime, then I fear you will be convicted.'

I was about to speak, but he raised his hand. 'But we can go into that later. First things first. Now, have you any money?'

'About a hundred and fifty pounds. But I haven't paid my hotel bill – I wasn't given the chance. I don't want hotel bilking to be added to the charge sheet, so it'll be nearer a hundred pounds I have to play around with.'

Maskell nodded. 'As you may know, my own fee has been taken care of. But I am not the man who will fight your case in court; that will be done by a barrister, and barristers come even more expensive than I do, especially barristers of the calibre needed to win this case. A hundred pounds would come nowhere near the amount necessary.'

I shrugged. 'I'm sorry; it's all I've got.' That wasn't exactly true but I could see that even the best barrister in the business couldn't get me out of this one and there wasn't any point in throwing my money away.

'I see. Well, there is provision for a case like yours. A barrister will be appointed by the Court to act for you. The trouble is that he will be not of your choice; yet I am not without influence and I will see if I have any strings to pull that will get us the best man.'

He took a folder from his briefcase and opened it. 'I want you to tell me exactly what you did on the morning in question.' He paused. 'I already know you did not have breakfast at your hotel.'

'I didn't sleep well that night,' I said. 'So I got up early and took a walk.'

Maskell sighed. 'And where did you walk to, Mr Rearden?'

I thought it out. 'I went into Hyde Park and walked up as far as the Round Pond. There's a famous building up there – Kensington Palace – but it was closed. It was very early in the morning.'

'I shouldn't imagine there would be many people in Hyde Park or Kensington Gardens so early. Did you speak to anyone – make enquiries – at Kensington Palace? Did you ask the time of opening, for instance?'

'There wasn't anyone around to ask.'

'Very well; what did you do then?'

'I walked back through the park to Hyde Park Corner and over into Green Park. Then up Bond Street into Oxford Street. I was doing a bit of window shopping, you see.'

'And what time would this be?'

'Oh, I don't know. Say, about nine-fifteen. I was daw-dling a bit. I had a look at a place called Burlington Arcade, then I went on up Bond Street looking at the shops, as I said. It's marvellous – nothing like it in South Africa.'

'And you didn't speak to anyone at all?'

'If I'd known I needed an alibi I would have,' I said bitterly.

'Just so,' said Maskell. 'So you arrived at Oxford Street – what did you do then?'

'Well, I hadn't had breakfast and I felt a bit peckish so I found a pub and had some sandwiches and a pint. I was chatting to the barman, an Irishman. He ought to remember me.'

'And what time was this?'

'It must have been after ten o'clock because the pub was open. Say, half past ten.'

'That alibi comes a little late,' said Maskell. 'It's not relevant.' He consulted a sheet of paper from the folder. 'I must tell you that the police version differs from yours substantially – and they have a great deal of evidence to show.' He looked me in the eye. 'Do I have to point out the dangers of lying to your lawyer?'

'I'm not lying,' I said indignantly.

He spoke gravely. 'Mr Rearden, let me say that you are in deep trouble. I gather you want to enter a plea of not guilty at your trial, but I must warn you that, on the evidence now extant, you are likely to lose the case. Public concern about crimes of violence of this nature has been increasing and this concern is reflected by the heavy sentences imposed by the courts.'

He paused to collect his thoughts and then went on in measured tones. 'Now, as your solicitor I cannot prejudge this case, but I would like to say this: If the diamonds were to be returned, and if you entered a plea of guilty, then the court would be inclined to leniency and, in my opinion, your sentence would be not more than five years and possibly as little as three years. With a remittance of sentence for good behaviour you could be out of prison in as little as two years.

'On the other hand, if the diamonds are *not* returned and if you enter a plea of not guilty then your sentence is going to be very heavy – assuming you are convicted, an assumption which on the evidence I have is very likely. If I may use slang I would say that his Lordship is going to throw the book at you; he'll lock you up and throw away the key. I doubt if you would get away with much under fourteen years, and I assure you that I have great experience in these forecasts and I do not speak lightly.'

He cleared his throat. 'Now, what do you say, Mr Rearden? What shall we do about this?'

'The only diamonds I saw that morning were in the shop windows of Bond Street,' I said distinctly.

He looked at me in silence for a long time then shook his head. 'Very well,' he said quietly. 'I will go about my business – and yours – but with no great hope of success. I ought to warn you that the police have such evidence that will be very difficult for defence counsel to refute.'

'I'm innocent,' I said obstinately.

He said no more but collected his papers and left the room without a backward glance.

II

So there I was in the dock of the Central Criminal Court – the Old Bailey. There was much pomp and circumstance, robes and wigs, deferences and courtesies – and me popping up from the bowels of the earth into the dock like the demon king in a pantomime, the centre of attraction. Of course, I had competition from the judge. It seems that when a man gets to sit on the Bench he feels that he's entitled to be a licensed jester and he loves nothing more than to have the audience rolling in the aisles at his witticisms. I've seen worse music hall turns than a Criminal Court judge. Still, it does lighten the atmosphere – a court would be a pretty grim place without the comic bits – and the Chief Comic isn't prejudiced; he aims his barbs at prosecution and defence alike. I found that I quite enjoyed it and laughed as much as anyone else.

Maskell was there, of course, but in a minor role; defence counsel was a man called Rollins. Maskell had tried again, just before the trial, to get me to alter my plea of not guilty. He said, 'Mr Rearden, I want you to consider once more the consequences of losing this case. You will not only receive a long sentence but there are certain other implications. Long-term prisoners are invariably regarded as high risk prisoners, especially those who are regarded as having financial backing. In the absence of diamonds to the value of £173,000 you would undoubtedly come into that category. A high risk prisoner is treated very differently from the ordinary prisoner and I understand that the circumstances can be rather unpleasant. I would think of that if I were you.'

I didn't have to think of it. I hadn't a hope in hell of getting the diamonds back and that was the crux of the matter. Even if I pleaded guilty I'd get a stiff sentence in the absence of the diamonds. The only thing to do was to put on a brave face and make the best of it. It struck me that Mackintosh was a very smart man and that maybe Mrs Smith was even smarter.

I said, 'I'm sorry, Mr Maskell, but I'm innocent.'

He looked puzzled. He didn't believe a word I said but he couldn't figure out why I was keeping my mouth shut. But then a wintry smile came to his face. 'I hope you don't think the investment of so many years of your life is worth the money. Too much time in prison is apt to change a man for the worse.'

I smiled at him. 'I thought you said you wouldn't prejudge the case.'

'I think you are a very foolish young man,' he said. 'But you have my best wishes in your unfortunate future.'

The trial got under way laboriously. First the jury details were settled and then the action began, the prosecution getting first crack. The prosecuting counsel was a tall, thin man with a face like the blade of a hatchet, and he fairly revelled in his job. He led off with a rather skimpy introduction and then began to lay on the prosecution witnesses, while Rollins, my counsel, looked on with a bored expression on his face. I had met Rollins only twice and he had been offhanded on both occasions. He knew this was one he wasn't going to win.

The prosecution witnesses were good – very good, indeed – and I began to see why the prosecuting counsel was looking so cheerful despite the misfortune of his face. Expert police witnesses introduced photographs and drawings of the scene of the crime and, that groundwork laid, the pressure was applied.

There was the motherly old soul who had identified me at the police station line-up. 'I saw him strike the postman,' she testified, the light of honesty shining from her eyes. 'I was standing in the corridor and saw the accused hit the postman with his fist, grab a yellow box from him, and push him into an office. Then the accused ran down the stairs.'

The prosecutor offered her a plan of the second floor. 'Where were you standing?'

She indicated a place in the corridor and looked across the court straight at me as guileless as you please. The sweet old lady was lying like a flatfish, and she knew that I knew she was lying. She couldn't have been standing in the corridor because I'd checked, and the details of her evidence were all wrong, anyway. There wasn't a thing I could do about it, though.

Another highlight was a man from Fortnum and Mason who testified to having sent a packed picnic basket to a certain hotel. The order was telephoned in by a Mr Rearden. Questioned by the defence he said he couldn't be certain that the Mr Rearden who ordered the basket was the accused.

A hotel employee testified that the accused stayed at his hotel and that a basket had been delivered addressed to Mr Rearden. Asked what had happened to it he said he didn't know but presumably the accused had collected it. There was a bit of argument about that and part of his answer was struck out.

A detective produced a picnic basket in court and testified that he had found it in the office of Kiddykar Toys Ltd. It had been identified as coming from Fortnum's. Another police witness testified that the basket was liberally covered with the accused's fingerprints, as were other items in the room; to wit – an electric kettle, a coffee pot and several pieces of crockery and cutlery.

The jury drew its own conclusions.

Then there was the police witness who said he had been interested in tracking down the ownership of Kiddykar Toys Ltd. Apparently it was a genuine company but not doing any business. The lines of ownership were very tangled but he had finally cracked it with the helpful assistance of the South African police. The owner proved to be a Mr Joseph Aloysius Rearden of Johannesburg. No, he had no means of knowing if the Joseph Aloysius Rearden of Kiddykars was the Joseph Aloysius Rearden who stood in the dock. That would be taking him further than he was prepared to go.

Again the jury drew its conclusions.

The postman gave his evidence fairly. I had hit him and he had recovered consciousness in the Kiddykar office.

There was nothing in that which contradicted the perjured evidence of Old Mother Hubbard. The third eye-witness was the office boy from Betsy-Lou; he said he saw me lock the office door and run downstairs. I remembered him vaguely as the person who had walked behind me at that time. But I hadn't *run* downstairs – that was his imagination working overtime.

Brunskill was a star witness.

'Acting on information received I went, with Detective-Sergeant Jervis, to see the accused at his hotel. His answers to my questioning were such that I arrested him on suspicion of having been concerned in this crime. Subsequently I obtained his fingerprints which matched prints found in the office of Kiddykar Toys Ltd. Further enquiries were made which resulted in three witnesses coming forward, all of whom identified the accused. More extensive enquiries led to the further evidence that has been presented to the Court relating to the picnic basket and the ownership of Kiddykar Toys Ltd.'

The prosecutor sat down with a grin on his face and Rollins bounced to his feet for cross-examination.

Rollins: You spoke of 'information received', Inspector. How did this information come to you?

Brunskill: (hesitantly) Must I answer that, my Lord? The sources of police information may be prejudicial to . . .

Rollins: (quickly) This goes to the malice of a person or persons unknown which may prejudice the case for the accused, my Lord.

Judge: (in Churchillian tones) Mr Rollins; I don't see how your case *can* deteriorate much further. However, I am inclined to let the question go. I am as interested as anybody. Answer the question, Inspector.

Brunskill: (unwillingly) There was one telephone call and one letter.

Rollins: Both anonymous?

Brunskill: Yes.

Rollins: Did these communications indicate that the accused had committed this crime?

Brunskill: Yes.

Rollins: Did they indicate where he was to be found?

Brunskill: Yes.

Rollins: Did they indicate that the basket found in the Kiddykar office had been purchased by the accused at Fortnum and Mason?

Brunskill: er . . . Yes.

Rollins: Is it a crime to purchase foodstuffs from that eminent firm of retailers?

Brunskill: (sharply) Of course not.

Rollins: Did these anonymous communications indicate that the firm of Kiddykar Toys Ltd was owned by the accused?

Brunskill: (uncomfortably) Yes.

Rollins: Is it a crime to own such a firm as Kiddykar Toys Ltd?

Brunskill: (with ebbing patience) No.

Judge: I am not so sure. Anyone who so maltreats the English language as to arrive at so abominable a name ought to be treated as a criminal.

(Laughter in court)

Rollins: Inspector, would you not say it was true that all your work had been done for you in this case? Would you not say it was true that without these malicious communications the accused would not be standing in the dock at this moment?

Brunskill: I cannot answer that question. He would have been caught.

Rollins: Would he? I admire your certitude.

Brunskill: He would have been caught.

Rollins: But not so speedily.

Brunskill: Perhaps not.

Rollins: Would you not characterize your mysterious communicant as someone who 'had it in' for the accused at worst – or a common informer or stool pigeon at best?

Brunskill: (smiling) I would prefer to think of him as a public-spirited citizen.

Very funny! Mackintosh – a public-spirited citizen! But, by God, the pair of them had been infernally clever. The first time I had laid eyes on that picnic basket had been in the Kiddykars office, and I certainly hadn't telephoned Fortnum's. Mrs Smith had done her shopping to good effect! Nor did I own Kiddykar Toys Ltd – not to my own knowledge; but I'd have a hell of a time proving it. They had delivered me to the law trussed up like a chicken.

There wasn't much after that. I said my piece, futile though it was; the prosecutor tore me into shreds and Rollins half-heartedly tried to sew up the pieces again without much success. The judge summed up and, with one careful eye on the Appeal Court, directed the jury to find me guilty. They were out only for half an hour – just time enough for a much-needed smoke – and the answer was predictable.

Then the judge asked if I had anything to say, so I spoke up with just two words: 'I'm innocent.'

Nobody took much notice of that – they were too busy watching the judge arrange his papers and gleefully anticipating how heavy he'd be. He fussed around for a while, making sure that all attention would be on him, and then he began to speak in portentous and doomladen tones.

'Joseph Aloysius Rearden, you have been found guilty of stealing by force diamonds to the value of £173,000. It falls to me to sentence you for this crime. Before I do so I would like to say a few words concerning your part in this affair.'

I could see what was coming. The old boy couldn't resist the chance of pontificating – it's easy from a safe seat.

'An Englishman is walking the streets in the course of his usual employ when he is suddenly and unexpectedly assaulted – brutally assaulted. He is not aware that he is carrying valuables which, to him, would undoubtedly represent untold wealth, and it is because of these valuables that he is attacked.

'The valuables – the diamonds – are now missing and you, Rearden, have not seen fit to co-operate with the police in their recovery in spite of the fact that you must have known that the court would be inclined to leniency had you done so. Therefore, you cannot expect leniency of this court.

'I have been rather puzzled by your recalcitrant attitude but my puzzlement abated when I made an elementary mathematical calculation. In the normal course of events such a crime as yours, a crime of violence such as is abhorrent in this country, coupled with the loss to the community of property worth £173,000, would be punished by the heavy sentence of fourteen years' imprisonment. My calculation, however, informs me that for those fourteen years you would be receiving an annual income of not less than £12,350 – tax free – being the amount you have stolen divided by fourteen. This, I might add, is considerably more than the stipend of one of Her Majesty's Judges, such as myself – a fact which can be ascertained by anyone who cares to consult Whitaker's Almanack.

'Whether it can be considered that the loss of fourteen years of freedom, and confinement to the hardly pleasant environs of our prisons, is worth such an annual sum is a debatable matter. You evidently think it is worth while. Now, it is not the function of this court to make the fees of crime worth while, so you can hardly blame me for endeavouring to reduce your annual prison income.

'Joseph Aloysius Rearden, I sentence you to twenty years' detention in such prison or prisons as the appropriate authority deems fit.'

I'd bet Mackintosh was laughing fit to bust a gut.

III

The judge was right when he referred to 'the hardly pleasant environs of our prisons'. The one in which I found myself was pretty deadly. The reception block was crowded – the judges must have been working overtime that day – and there was a lot of waiting about apparently pointlessly. I was feeling a bit miserable; no one can stand in front of a judge and receive a twenty year sentence with complete equanimity.

Twenty years!

I was thirty-four years old. I'd be fifty-four when I came out; perhaps a bit less if I could persuade them I was a good boy, but that would be bloody difficult in view of what the judge had said. Any Review Board I appeared before would read a transcript of the trial and the judge's remarks would hit them like a hammer.

Twenty long years!

I stood by apathetically while the police escort read out the details of my case to the receiving officer. 'All right,' said the receiving officer. He signed his name in a book and tore out a sheet. 'Here's the body receipt.'

So help me – that's what he said. 'Body receipt.' When you're in prison you cease to be a man; you're a body, a zombie, a walking statistic. You're something to be pushed around like the GPO pushed around that little yellow box containing the diamonds; you're a parcel of blood and guts that needs feeding at regular intervals, and you're assumed not to have any brains at all.

'Come on, you,' said the receiving officer. 'In here.' He unlocked a door and stood aside while I walked in. The door slammed behind me and I heard the click of the lock. It was a crowded room filled with men of all types, judging

46

by their clothing. There was everything from blue jeans to a bowler and striped trousers. Nobody was talking – they just stood around and examined the floor minutely as though it was of immense importance. I suppose they all felt like me; they'd had the wind knocked out of them.

We waited in that room for a long time, wondering what was going to happen. Perhaps some of us knew, having been there before. But this was my first time in an English gaol and I felt apprehensive. Maskell's words about the unpleasant circumstances that attend the high risk prisoner began to worry me.

At last they began to take us out, one at a time and in strict alphabetical order. Rearden comes a long way down the alphabet so I had to wait longer than most, but my turn came and a warder took me down a passage and into an office.

A prisoner is never asked to sit down. I stood before that desk and answered questions while a prison officer took down the answers like the recording angel. He took down my name, birthplace, father's name, mother's maiden name, my age, next-of-kin, occupation. All that time he never looked at me once; to him I wasn't a man, I was a statistics container – he pressed a button and the statistics poured out.

They told me to empty my pockets and the contents were dumped on to the desk and meticulously recorded before being put into a canvas bag. Then my fingerprints were taken. I looked around for something with which to wipe off the ink but there was nothing. I soon found out why. A warder marched me away and into a hot, steamy room where I was told to strip. It was there I lost my clothes. I wouldn't see them again for twenty years and I'd be damned lucky if they'd be in fashion.

After the bath, which wasn't bad, I dressed in the prison clothing – the man in the grey flannel suit. But the cut was terrible and I'd rather have gone to Mackintosh's tailor.

A march up another corridor led to a medical examination, a bit of bureaucratic stupidity. Why they can't have a medical examination while a man is stripped after his bath is beyond me. However, I undressed obligingly and dressed again, and was graded for labour. I was top class – fit for anything.

Then a warder took me away again into an immense hall with tiers of cells lining the walls and with iron stairs like fire escapes. 'I'll tell you once,' said the warder. 'This is "C" Hall.'

We clanked up some stairs and along a landing and he stopped before a cell and unlocked it. 'This is yours.'

I went inside and the door slammed with a cold sound of finality. I stood for some time, not looking at anything in particular. My brains had seized up – gone on strike. After, maybe, fifteen minutes I lay on the bed and damn near cried my eyes out.

After that I felt better and was able to bring some intelligence to bear on the situation. The cell was about twelve feet by seven, and perhaps eight feet high. The walls were distempered – institutional cream and Borstal green – and in one of them was a small barred window set high. The door looked as though it could withstand artillery fire and there was a Judas hole set in it.

The furnishing was sparse; an iron-framed bed, a wooden table and a chair, a washstand with a jug, basin and chamber-pot, and a bare shelf. Exploring a prison cell is one of the quickest tasks a man can set himself. Within three minutes I had checked everything there was to find – three blankets, two sheets, a lumpy mattress, another shirt, a pair of felt slippers, a thin non-absorbent towel, a spoon and a mug. Hanging on a nail in the wall by a loop of string was a copy of the Rules and Regulations governing HM Prisons together with an informational pamphlet.

Three minutes and I knew practically everything there was to know about that cell. I wondered what I was going to do for the next twenty years. Right there and then I decided I'd have to ration my curiosity – shut down the dampers on thought. There would be too much time and not enough happening, and every new experience would have to be jealously hoarded.

The walls of that prison suddenly had physical meaning. I felt them looming all about me, thick and strong. It was a claustrophobic quarter-hour before the feeling receded and I was able to stop shivering.

I immediately broke my promise about rationing curiosity by beginning to read the informational pamphlet, but that was absolutely necessary. I was a new boy in this school and the sooner I learned the ropes the better. There were too many tricks that could be played on the newcomer by the old hands and I didn't want to fall for any of them.

It was an interesting compilation of data. I discovered that the spare shirt in the cell was to be used as a night shirt, that lights-out was ten-thirty, that the waking call was six-thirty in the morning, that I was to be issued with a razor blade to be returned after shaving. There were other helpful hints even to the point of finding a way out of prison.

For instance, I could refer my case to the Court of Criminal Appeal and, if that failed, I could apply to the Attorney-General to put the case before the House of Lords. At any time I could petition the Home Secretary and I was permitted to write to my Member of Parliament.

I couldn't see myself doing any of those things. I wasn't pally enough with the Home Secretary to enter into any kind of extended correspondence and my Member of Parliament was a shade too far away to do any good – 6,000 miles away.

I read the booklet through and then started on it again from the beginning. I had nothing else to do so I decided to memorize the whole goddamn thing. I was still reading it when the light went out.

IV

The bell clanged and I opened my eyes and was confused until I remembered where I was. I dressed hurriedly and made the bed, then hoisted it up so that it stood on end in a corner of the cell. I sat on the chair and waited. Presently there was a slight metallic sound from the door and I knew someone was watching through the Judas hole.

There was a sharp snap from the lock and the door opened. I stood up and the warder came in. He looked appraisingly around the cell and then fixed me with a hard eye. 'You're new here. You've been reading that thing, haven't you?' He nodded to the booklet on the table.

'Yes, I have.'

'Your bed's in the wrong corner, and the book should be hanging on the wall where you found it. You'll learn. Take a tip from me; do just what you're told and you'll be all right. Now, pick up your chamber-pot and get ready for slopping out.'

'I haven't used it,' I said.

'It gets slopped out whether you've used it or not,' he said curtly. 'Remember what I told you – do as you're told with no arguments. That's lesson number one.'

I picked up the chamber-pot and followed him on to the landing which was full of men, all lined up and each holding his pot. 'All right,' someone shouted. 'Move along.'

There was mephitic stink in the air. I trudged along and found that I was expected to empty the pot into one sink and wash it in another. I went through the motions and returned to my cell, taking my cues from what the others were doing.

The warder came back. 'You can eat in your cell if you like. You'll be served with the others down in the hall, but